John Newton Stearns

The Juvenile Temperance Reciter

A Collection of Recitations and Declamations

John Newton Stearns

The Juvenile Temperance Reciter
A Collection of Recitations and Declamations

ISBN/EAN: 9783337371654

Printed in Europe, USA, Canada, Australia, Japan

Cover: Foto ©Andreas Hilbeck / pixelio.de

More available books at **www.hansebooks.com**

THE

JUVENILE TEMPERANCE RECITER:

A COLLECTION

OF

RECITATIONS AND DECLAMATIONS,

IN PROSE AND VERSE,

FOR USE IN

BANDS OF HOPE, JUVENILE TEMPLES, TEMPERANCE
SCHOOLS, SUNDAY-SCHOOLS, AND ALL
JUVENILE ORGANIZATIONS.

NEW YORK:
The National Temperance Society and Publication House,
58 READE STREET.

—

1880.

CONTENTS.

PROSE.

POETRY.

What to Drink.

GEO. S. BURLEIGH.

THE Lily drinks the sunlight,
  The Primrose drinks the dew,
The Cowslip sips the running brook,
  The Hyacinth heaven's blue.

The Peaches quaff the dawnlight,
  The Pears the autumn noon,
The Apple-blossoms drink the rain
  And the first warm air of June.

The Wind-flower and the Violet
  Draw in the April breeze,
And sun, and rain, and hurricane
  Are the tipple of the trees.

But not a bud or greenling,
  From the Hyssop on the wall
To the Cedars of Mount Lebanon,
  Is steeped in alcohol.

From all earth's emerald basin,
  From the blue sky's sapphire bowl,
No living thing of root or wing
  Partakes that deadly dole.

5

I'll quaff the Lily's nectar,
  I'll sip at the Cowslip's cup,
I'll drink the shower, the sun, the breeze,
  But never a poisoned drop.

Something to be Done.

MARY D. CHELLIS.

THERE'S a battle to be fought,
  A victory to be gained ;
There's a country to be saved,
  A host from sin reclaimed.

There's an enemy abroad,
  So subtle and so strong
That the conflict must be fierce,
  The struggle must be long.

We're recruiting for the ranks
  For years and years to come,
That our numbers may not fail
  Ere triumph shall be won.

" Sample-Room."

[THIS IS A NEW NAME FOR A GROG-SHOP.]

VIRGINIA J. KENT.

" SAMPLE " of a daughter, brother,
  Lured to ruin, sin, and shame ;
"Sample " of a father, mother,
  Lost to reason, right, and fame !

" Sample " of the red wine mocker,
  " Sample " of the serpent's sting,
"Sample " of a midnight murder,
  " Sample " of each cursèd thing !

"Sample" of all woes for ever,
  "Sample" of all sorrows known,
"Sample" of all vain endeavor,
  "Sample" of God's image flown !

"Sample"—not of manhood's greatness ;
  "Sample"—not the godlike fear ;
But of vice and all uncleanness,
  Vengeance, fury, and despair!

God's Work.

ELLA WHEELER.

GATHERING brands from the burning,
  Plucking them out of the fire,
Lifting the sheep that have wandered
  Out of the dust and the mire ;
Bringing home sheaves from the harvest,
  To lay at the Master's feet—
Lord, all thy hosts of angels
  Must smile on a life so sweet.

Speaking with fear of no man,
  Speaking with love for all,
Warning the young and thoughtless
  From the wild beast, "Alcohol ";
Showing the snares that the tempter
  Weaveth on every hand—
Lord, all thy dear, dear angels
  Must smile on a life so grand.

Fighting the bloodless battle
  With a heart that is true and bold—
Fighting it not for glory,
  Fighting it not for gold,

But out of love for his neighbor,
  And out of love for his Lord ;
I know that the hands of the angels
  Will crown him with his reward.

For whoso works for the Master,
  And whoso fights His fight,
The angel's crown with a star-wreath ;
  And it glows with gems most bright.
They wear them for ever and ever,
  The saints in that land of bliss,
And I know that heaven's best jewel
  Is kept for a soul like this.

A Call for Recruits.

(As the speaker advances to the platform, some boy should beat a drum, and stop as he completes his first sentence.)

HARK ! the drum is beating for recruits.   Who will volunteer to take up arms and fight against this awful demon ?   His name is Alcohol, or Strong Drink, and the fearful amount of crime, misery, pauperism, lunacy, and death which he has caused, and is still causing, calls aloud to every friend of humanity to act a brother's part and come "to the help of the Lord against the mighty !"   Though the foe is great, and has a mighty power, the painful ravages of this monster shall not continue for ever.   There shall come a time when God's glory shall "cover the earth as the waters cover the sea."   If it were not so the Saviour would never have taught us to pray : "Our Father which art in heaven, hallowed be Thy name ; Thy kingdom come ; Thy will be done on earth, as it is in heaven."   And when that glorious time shall come there will not be a drunkard nor dram-shop on the face of the whole world.   Is it not worth your while, then,

to help on that glad time ? Will you not come and
help us in this warfare, and take up arms for the de-
fence and the redemption of our country, and by every
means in your power attempt to banish this crying
evil from our midst ?

In the name of suffering humanity we appeal to
each and all of you to set your faces against, and use
your influence to pull down and root up for ever, the
drinking customs of our land. Will you not enlist
yourselves on our side ?

Strike for Prohibition.

STRIKE for prohibition ;
    Ask for nothing less ;
Labor for its triumph,
    Pray for its success.

Put it in your school-books ;
    Teach it to the young ;
Let it be the key-note
    Of the nation's song.

Sound it from the pulpit,
    Through the public press ;
Speed it on its mission,
    Every home to bless.

With its holy incense
    Burden ev'ry breeze
From Lake Superior's waters
    To the Southern Seas.

Waft it on the zephyrs
    Over ev'ry State,
From Atlantic's borders
    To the Golden Gate.

Onward let the echoes
  Roll from shore to shore,
Heralding the demon
  Banished evermore !

Temperance.

MORE of good than we can tell,
More to buy with, more to sell ;
More of comfort, less of care,
More to eat and more to wear ;
Happier homes, with faces brighter,
All our burdens rendered lighter ;
Conscience clean and minds much stronger,
Debts much shorter, purses longer ;
Hopes that drive away all sorrow,
And something laid up for to-morrow.

A Water-Drinker's Song.

FRED SHERLOCH.

LET those who will
  Go drink their fill
Of ale, or beer, or wine, boys !
  'Twill better pay,
  I boldly say,
To keep to water fine, boys !
  With muddled head
  In danger led,
The toper comes to grief, sirs ;
  But water bright
  Will keep one right
And strong, is my belief, sirs.

Take away care,
The foe beware,
Refuse the tempting dram, sirs ;
True courage gain,
Like men abstain,
And steady keep the brain, sirs ;
With heart and nerve
Your country serve,
Beat down the lust of greed, boys !
'Tis not by gold,
But purpose bold,
The nation shall be freed, boys.

———

The Band of Hope Pledge.

THERE'S *danger* in the *drink*, boys,
  It's led good men astray ;
There's *safety* in the *pledge*, boys,
  It leads in the safe way.

There's *mischief* in the *drink*, boys,
  We see it every day ;
There's *power* in the *pledge*, boys,
  To drive the sin away.

There are *squabbles* in the *drink*, boys—
  Just hear the drunkard swear ;
There's *order* in the *pledge*, boys,
  We see it everywhere.

There's *mockery* in the *drink*, boys,
  The adder's sting is there ;
There's *wisdom* in the *pledge*, boys—
  Keep it by " faith and prayer."

There's *falsehood* in the *drink*, boys ;
  How many it has grieved !
There's *justice* in the *pledge*, boys ;
  None has it wronged—deceived.

There's *sadness* in the *drink*, boys,
  It wrings the head with pain ;
There's *gladness* in the *pledge*, boys,
  If you will aye abstain.

There's *discord* in the *drink*, boys,
  And "brawls" of every kind.
There's *concord* in the *pledge*, boys ;
  About thy neck *it* bind.

There's *ruin* in the *drink*, boys ;
  How many it has killed !
There's *beauty* in the *pledge*, boys ;
  With joy my heart it's filled.

Good Habits.

JAMES H. KELLOGG.

IF a man is only a "bundle of habits,"
  And the habits the growth of years,
Of working or shirking, dreaming or scheming,
  Of loves, and hates, and fears—

Then a boy should begin with such habits
  As are just, and manly, and right ;
He should learn to hate the false and the wrong,
  And in good to take delight.

He should speak the truth in holy love,
  And help his needy brother ;
The Lord has promised a rich reward
  For the good we do each other.

He should try to be both gentle and meek,
And joyful and faithful, too ;
In every place and at every time
To be kind, and respectful, and true.

The habit of sipping wine or beer,
Or drinking whiskey or gin
When "hot or cold, when wet or when dry,"
I hope you will *never begin.*

Say *no!* when you're offered the first tempting glass,
And say it so firmly, too,
That the boy or the man who hands you the drink
Will find something better to do.

I would sign the pledge on my next birthday,
And keep it for all my life ;
This will save you a world of trouble and care,
And woe, and sorrow, and strife.

The Invader.

A CRY of agony rings throughout our country.
East, West, North, and South echo the sad refrain.   It
comes from broken, widowed hearts and with orphan
tears ; the awful wail of lost souls swells the dismal
chorus.   Why are these lamentations heard around
us ?   Because a demon has invaded our once happy
land, spreading death, desolation, and misery on every
hand.   He promises fair, yet his promises are but
cheating lies to lure his victims to destruction.   To
him the words of the Psalmist might be well applied :
"He hath laid his hand upon such as be at peace with
him, he hath broken his covenant ; the words of his
mouth are softer than butter, but war is in his heart ;
his words are smoother than oil, yet they are drawn

swords." Under the guise of truest friendship he
drags his victims down to vice, sorrow, and death in
this world, and eternal ruin in the next. None are
so rich that they are above the grasp of his destructive
power ; none so poor but they become his victims.
He destroys our homes, breaks up our happiness, sow-
ing strife and discord in thousands of families, and
carries away the fairest victims. Our jails, asylums,
and poor-houses are filled by his influence. In almost
every city, town, and village, as well as by the high-
way side, he spreads his nets, that the unwary may
fall therein. He clothes himself in a variety of guises
and assumes a variety of names, but whatever the
guise or name, the same evil spirit pervades his
whole nature. He is a vile deceiver.

Little Drops.

LITTLE drops of claret,
  Now and then, at first,
Form an awful habit
  And a dreadful thirst.

Little drinks of lager,
  Little cups of ale,
Make the biggest guzzler—
  Never knew it fail.

Little kegs of whiskey
  Often brought from town,
Make a man a monkey,
  Or a silly clown.

Little drops of brandy,
  Little drops of rye,
Make the mighty toper
  And the watery eye.

Do Thy Little.

Do thy little—do it well ;
Do what right and reason tell ;
Do what wrong and sorrow claim—
Conquer sin and cover shame.

Do thy little, though it be
Dreariness and drudgery ;
They whom Christ apostles made
"Gathered fragments" when He bade.

Do thy little.   God hath made
Million leaves for forest shade ;
Smallest stars their glory bring ;
God employeth everything.

Do thy little ; and when thou
Feelest on thy pallid brow,
Ere has fled the vital breath,
Cold and damp, the sweat of death,

Then the little thou hast done—
Little battles thou hast won,
Little masteries achieved,
Little wants with care relieved,
Little words in love expressed,
Little wrongs at once confessed,
Little favors kindly done,
Little toils thou didst not shun,
Little graces meekly won,
Little slights with patience borne—

These shall crown thy pillowed head,
Holy light upon thee shed ;
These are treasures that shall rise
Far beyond the shining skies.

Drink Not a Drop.

If I would not be a drunkard,
  I must not drink a drop
Of wine, that looks so tempting
  Within the ruby cup ;
For such a small beginning,
  Though innocent it seem,
May lead me on to sinning
  More fearful than I dream.

If I would not be a drunkard,
  I stoutly must refuse
All the sorts of beer and cider
  Which other people use.
They may not steal my reason,
  But they will give the taste,
And lead me on when older
  To drinking all the rest.

Not One Step Backward.

R. THOMPSON.

Not one step backward ; ever on,
  Till the great temp'rance victory's won,
We'll press our way and boldly fight,
  Strong in the confidence of right.

Not one step backward ; on we'll go
  Till drunkenness, our common foe,
Receives a last, a mortal thrust,
  And lies expiring in the dust.

Not one step backward ; onward still
  We'll press with firm, determined will,
Till age like youth are free
  From drink's enslaving tyranny.

Not one step backward ; still we'll on
Till all our fellows, every one,
Are freed from its debasing thrall
And temperance is the rule of all.

What a Pity!

WHAT a pity people drink,
    Losing all their senses !
If they would but try to think,
    They wouldn't have such fancies.

For what is ale or porter,
    Making heads to ache ?
It is but poisoned water,
    Making nerves to shake

Will you now, my friends, allow
    A little boy's advice ?
You'll never have a drunken row
    In your teetotal house.

I beg that you the pledge will take,
    And throw the drink away ;
Do it for your children's sake,
    And do it right away.

Don't Begin.

IF you would not be a swearer,
                Don't begin ;
In the first low-uttered oath
                Lies the sin !
If you would not be a drunkard,
                Don't begin ;
In the first glass lies your danger—
                Don't begin !

Speech for a Band of Hope Boy.

FOR AN ANNUAL FESTIVAL.

A. J. GLASSPOOL.

MR. CHAIRMAN, ladies and gentlemen : I should not venture to address to you any remarks this evening were I not convinced that you will grant me the greatest indulgence, and cheerfully forgive any errors into which I may fall. It might be expected, on such a happy occasion as this, some information would be given to visitors as to the object and work of our Band of Hope. I think I may be forgiven if I say that our object is a noble one, since we endeavor to prevent the children falling into a well-known, and which all admit to be one of the greatest evils of our day—I mean the evil of drunkenness.

Mr. Chairman, you will excuse me, therefore, naming our society a preventive society. Our Committee look around, and they find that many persons become paupers, criminals, or lunatics through the drinking of intoxicating liquors ; and they find also that these persons learned to drink when they were young. Our Committee then wisely determined to use some means to protect the children of our day from such a terrible end. To accomplish this good result we are invited to meet together week by week ; with the consent of our parents we have made a promise never to taste a drop of intoxicating liquor as beverages, and, in order to encourage and help us to keep that promise, at our weekly meetings we are instructed in the nature and properties of strong drinks, and by earnest prayer to our Heavenly Father we are made strong to bear ridicule, and to hold fast to our promise against every temptation.

Some persons might fear that if the children were taught to abstain from intoxicating drinks, they might suffer in bodily and mental strength, or lose their position in society ; but, ladies and gentlemen, you will, I am convinced, agree with me when I say that such results have never been found. I appeal to every one present this evening whether the bright eyes and the rosy cheeks of our Band of Hope members are not equal in appearance to any that children who drink moderately can show. I am quite certain of one fact, that the ladies who preside at the tea-tables are quite agreed that our teetotalism has not taken away our appetites or robbed us of good digestions. We are quite sure that we are better in body and mind, and in every respect, than those who are exposed to the temptation of the drink.

Let us take courage ; under the banner of temperance the great and noble are now gathering. We follow in the footsteps of good and brave men whose names will live for ever. At our head we behold John Wesley, the pious and industrious minister ; Sir Henry Havelock, the soldier of India ; Sir John Ross, the explorer of the Arctic seas ; and many other glorious names, who in one voice bid us hold faithfully to the pledge. If, ladies and gentlemen, you will help us by your example and by your kind gifts, we shall feel encouraged to continue in this good work. Allow me, Mr. Chairman, ladies and gentlemen, to thank you very much for your kind attention to my few remarks.

Queer Medicines.

MRS. M. A. KIDDER.

"I 'M dry," says the glutton,
    " As dry as a fish ;
  So give me a 'bumper'
  To season my dish."

" I'm wet," says the traveller ;
   " I fain would be dry.
  Prepare for my comfort
   A glass of ' old rye.' "

"I'm cold ! almost frozen ;
   So build up a fire
  In shape of a ' rum-punch,'
   To make me perspire."

"I'm hot," says the other,
   "From toe unto crown.
  I'd fain have a ' julep'
   To cool my blood down."

And so men will swallow,
   To patch up their ills
  And change their condition,
   The devil's worst pills.

I'm Teetotal, I Assure You.

FOR A SMALL BOY.

I'M a little tiny thing,
   But I'm teetotal, I assure you,
  And I'm not ashamed to bring
   This subject now before you.

Many little ones are taught
   To love the drunkard's drink, sir ;
  And when they've grown they've soon been
     brought
   To beggary and want, sir.

To prison and the hangman's drop—
   The drink has done all this, sir ;
  Before the dupes themselves would stop
   They've sacrificed their lives, sir.

I know I'm on the winning side ;
    Drink will not master me, sir.
I *feel* I am my mother's pride ;
    Drink will ne'er break *her heart*, sir.

I'll fight the monster, *that* I will—
    I have a sword for this, sir ;
I'll *drink the water from the rill*,
    And that will stab him through, sir.

I'm only now a little man,
    But when I am full grown, sir,
I'll *beard* the monster in his den,
    And follow up the blow, sir.

The Rumseller's Song.

REV. CHAS. WHEELER DENISON.

THE rumseller sat in his den alone,
Singing his thoughts in an undertone.
Shrouded in silence, his work was done
Since the rise and set of the daily sun.
He had squared his books ; he had counted his gains ;
Then he startled the night with his spirited strains ;
And he sang as he hoarded his wages of sin :
    "I gather them in ! I gather them in !
            Gather ! gather ! gather !
        I gather them in !

"The old with their thin and frosty hair,
The young with ringlets dark and fair,
The smiling bridegroom and the bride,
The brother and sister, side by side,
Captive and bound in the toils I spread ;
On to their doom my victims tread—
Stranger and neighbor, alien, kin,
    I gather them in ! I gather them in !

"The statesman, the orator, learned and proud,
The tramp in the rags of the dirty crowd,
The toiler on land, the child of the sea,
By thousands and thousands come trooping to me !
In the golden ray of the morning light,
In the darkness, and stillness, and dead of night,
From the desert waste, from the city's din,
   I gather them in ! I gather them in!

"Through all ages of time, through all regions of
     space,
I trade in the blood of the human race !
My license to kill is all free from a flaw,
For the votes of good Christians enacted the law !
The ballots of party I hold in my hand,
And the leaders are hacks to obey my command !"
So the rumseller sang of his wages of sin :
   "I gather them in ! I gather them in !
      Gather ! gather ! gather !
      Gather them in !"

Strength for To-day.

STRENGTH for to-day is all that we need,
   As there never will be a to-morrow ;
For to-morrow will prove but another to-day,
   With its measure of joy and sorrow.

Then why forecast the trials of life
   With such sad and grave persistence,
And watch and wait for a crowd of ills
   That as yet have no existence ?

Strength for to-day—what a precious boon
   For the earnest souls who labor,
For the willing hands that minister
   For the needy friend or neighbor !

Strength for to-day—that the weary hearts
In the battle for right may quail not,
And the eyes bedimmed with bitter tears
In their search for light may fail not.

Strength for to-day—on the downhill track,
For the travellers near the valley,
That up, far up, the other side
Ere long they may safely rally.

Strength for to-day—that our precious youth
May happily shun temptation,
And build, from the rise to the set of the sun,
On a strong and sure foundation.

Strength for to-day—in house and home
To practise forbearance sweetly ;
To scatter kind words and loving deeds,
Still trusting in God completely.

The Children's Pledge.

THIS little band do with our hand
The pledge now sign to drink no wine ;
Nor brandy red, to turn our head ;
Nor crazy gin, to tempt to sin ;
Nor whiskey hot, that makes the sot ;
Nor ale nor beer, to make us queer ;
Nor fiery rum, to turn our home
Into a hell where none could dwell ;
Where peace would fly, where hope would die,
And love expire 'mid such a fire.
To quench our thirst we'll always bring
Cold water from the well or spring ;
So here we pledge perpetual hate
To all that can intoxicate.

A Fool's Excuse.

G. W. BUNGAY.

HE who drinks when he's hot
To keep himself cool,
Adds the vice of the sot
To the deed of a fool !
He who drinks when he's cool
To keep himself hot,
Adds the deed of a fool
To the vice of a sot.

Never Give Up.

NEVER give up, children ; don't say, "I won't," or "I can't," but instead say, "I'll try, any way, and succeed if possible." Don't be like the negligent school-boy who takes his book to work out a problem, but soon throws it down, saying, " I can't understand that ; why do I try ? I cannot waste my precious time here ; I ought to be out of doors snowballing." And so off he goes, feeling very much injured that his teacher should wish him to destroy his health by studying arithmetic when he ought to be exercising in the open air. Yes, there is the excuse—a worn one, by the way—that scholars often make to themselves, to crush down their conscience, which *will* sometimes rebuke notwithstanding.

Don't surrender at trifles. I suppose you have all read of the prince who went to seek his fortune once upon a time, and was obliged to hew down masses of rock as high as mountains that lay in his pathway ; but he succeeded, building castles and founding cities, because he never gave up, and at last was made king of the world.

Now if you will hew down the rock "I can't," and build up the castle "I'll try," never fear but that you will be made king, not of the world, but of yourself, which I think is much better. You will not then be likely to throw your books into one corner, while you sit in another, feeling very unreasonable, and ready to fly into a passion at the slightest provocation, all because you have said, "I can't learn my lesson, and what is more, I won't try!"

Don't be dismayed at obstacles. They are things that *will* come up before us, and they *must* be *overcome*. Remember with what small means great things have been accomplished, and remember, too, that it is within your power to do nearly, if not quite, as well, providing that you will say, "I will never give up!"

The Inebriate's Ladder.

MRS. C. H. OBEAR.

THE inebriate's ladder
  I'll describe, my dear friends,
Round by round from the top
  (For it never ascends).
The first round is cider,
  With perhaps some home-wine ;
Tobacco with these two
  Will often combine.

The next round, *hard* cider,
  With strong beer or ale,
Or now and then whiskey,
  If you're feeble and pale.
Once your foot on this round
  Your relish is gone
For pure, simple drinks,
  And ill turns oft come on.

Soon you crave something stronger ;
  The next lower round
You will find gin and brandy,
  At first weakened down ;
But your thirst still increases,
" You *must* quaff at a bowl
Not diluted or weakened,
  If it ruins your soul."

Another step down
  You will find the pure *rum ;*
And when *that* step's taken,
  To the last you have come !
Below you the pit !
  And you stand there *alone—*
Health, home, and happiness
  Evermore gone !

Be Steady.

Be steady, boys ; whate'er you do
Remember the pledge to keep in view,
And whether belonging to red or blue,
  Be steady.

Remember, boys, 'tis hard to bear
The scoffs, abuse, the slurs, the care
That we are called upon to share—
  Be steady.

Just think of the army in the field,
Before whom Alcohol must yield ;
Then wear your ribbon for a shield—
  Be steady.

Then stand up manly in the fight,
Until Satan's hosts are put to flight ;
Your cause is just, you're in the right—
  Be steady.

Then be steady, boys ; whate'er you do
Remember the pledge to keep in view ;
We belong to an army that's brave and true—
  Be steady.

Only a Boy.

" I am only a boy ! " did you say ?
  Well, yes ; I am only a boy—
A boy full of mischievous play.
  Let me ask, Were you ever a boy ?

I am only a boy ! What of that ?
  I shall grow, if I live, to a man ;
I shall throw away tops, ball and bat,
  And work on a definite plan.

I am only a boy, it is true ;
  It would do you more good, sir, by far,
To romp about now as I do
  Than to puff at that sickly cigar.

I'm a Band of Hope boy, sir ; I've signed
  The pledge to abstain from strong drink ;
And there's many a man I could find
  Would do well to do that, sir, I think.

Yes, there's many a man that I know
  Would do better to act in that way
Than to win to himself boundless wealth,
  For wealth would but lead him astray.

I am only a boy, it is true,
  But I'm going to do what I can ;
And if I do that, sir, why, you
  Will believe I shall make a good man.

I shall fight for the right while I can,
  And my talents and time well employ ;
If I would be a temperance man,
  Why, I must be a temperance boy.

Rallying Song of the Temperance Army.

WE are marshalling the forces
  Of an army true and strong ;
We are marching to the music
  Of a ringing temperance song ;
We are going forth to battle
  With a hydra-headed wrong,
Till one grand, triumphant chorus
  Shall the victors' shout prolong!

Where the bugle calls to battle—
  If Heaven that call repeat—
If right and duty lead us,
  There alone the path is sweet!
Though the proud may deem this service
  Both for us and them unmeet,
Unheeding scorn or frowning,
  We will go with fearless feet!

We are pledged to guard each other,
  And all those we love the best,
From the poisoned darts and arrows
  Of a fell destroyer's quest!

And our battle-cry is "Onward !
  No faltering and no rest
Till his flaunting, mocking ensign
  In dishonored dust is pressed ! "

With hearts aglow with pity
  For the tempted ones we fall,
And with arms outstretched to rescue
  Wounded friend or foe, or all.
We are pledged to do our utmost
  To break down this tyrant's thrall ;
Ne'er "Am I my brother's keeper ? "
  Be *our* answer to God's call!

See, bright from many a hill-top
  New camp-fires flash and glow ;
From rank and file and tented field
  Hear songs of victory go !
Shout answers shout—a wave of sound
  Breaks in impetuous flow—
"All hail!" "What cheer ?" " 'Tis morning";
  " We are conquering the foe!"

A Little Girl's Speech.

THEY thought I couldn't make a speech,
  I'm such a little tot ;
I'll show them whether I can do
  A thing or two, or not.

Don't be afraid to fight the wrong,
  Or stand up for the right ;
And when you've nothing else to say,
  Be sure you say—good-night.

Four Reasons.

A. J. GLASSPOOL.

This may be used as well for any other organization, by changing the words " Band of Hope " to the name of the Society.

MR. CHAIRMAN, ladies and gentlemen : I have been asked by our secretary to say a few words to you this evening. I must first say that I feel myself quite unable to say anything to those who are so much older than your humble servant; I shall therefore, with your kind permission, Mr. Chairman, say a few words to the members of our Band of Hope, who are here in good numbers this evening ; but their numbers do not surprise me, for the members are naturally anxious to be present to show their sympathy with the Band of Hope work.

Fellow-members, why have we acted wisely in joining this Band of Hope ? I will give you four reasons why, in my humble opinion, we have done right. First, we are right in joining the Band of Hope, because we want to save MONEY. If we have any money to spend, we want to spend it in that which will feed the body, clothe the back, or educate the mind. Intoxicating drinks cannot do any of these good things ; they cannot give strength, they are only a false stimulant, they never act as a food, they only create an appetite for themselves. The drinking of intoxicating liquors often makes the drinker indifferent as to the clothes he wears, for the money paid to the publican had better be paid to the draper and the tailor. Intoxicating liquors are useless for brain-work, and those who take them for that purpose injure the brain and in time destroy the mental faculties. Fellow-members, when we are older we want to be our own landlords, and if we save the same amount of money that many of our rela-

lives spend on the drink we shall in the future be able
to bid the landlord good-by and have money in the
bank to spend in old age. Secondly, we have done
right in joining the Band of Hope, because we want to
save our HEALTH. Some of our members have been
abstainers all their lives ; I venture to say that those
of our parents who have trained us in temperance ways
have nothing to complain of in regard to our health.
Our strength is good, our tongues are never quiet, and
our appetites are very remarkable. We want to pre-
serve this beautiful gift of health ; we know that the
drinking of intoxicating liquors not only takes away
health, but also destroys life. Thirdly, we have done
rightly in signing the pledge, because we want to save
CHARACTER. The boy who seeks a situation without a
character will find it very difficult to obtain a good
master. A good character is more valuable than either
wealth or health. Let us seek to keep this important
blessing. No one can deny that a master would rather
employ a man who can be trusted always to be present
at the hour of commencing business than a man whose
bad habits keep him up late at night, and send him to
business late the next morning. Who, then, can de-
serve the confidence of his employer better than the
man who, abstaining from strong drinks, and from
places where the drink is sold, retires to rest early and
is up with the lark in the morning ?

We make no boast, but it cannot be denied that
total abstainers are seldom seen in the prisoners' dock
at the police court, and their characters are generally
free from crime or debt.

I will trouble you, Mr. Chairman, with but one
more reason, and this last one shall be the most important of all. We all want to obtain wealth, health, and
good character, but above all we desire to save our

souls. Total abstinence will not open the gate of heaven to us, but under its influence we shall form such associations that our thoughts will be directed to spiritual things, and we shall find joy by attending the church and the Sunday-school. Ladies and gentlemen, I will not trouble you with any more reasons ; I will conclude this short address with the following lines :

" To save the cash, to save my brains,
　　To break each slavish link,
　To have a hope of heaven at last,
　　I never touch the drink.

" I'm sure you think my reasons good;
　　My earnest words don't blame.
　You think 'tis good for *me* to sign:
　　Why don't *you* do the same? "

Independence Day.

(A SPEECH FOR THE FOURTH OF JULY.)

REV. MR. PIERPONT was one of the poets of the early days of the reform. On July 4, 1839, the law being on the side of temperance in Boston, a great jubilee meeting was held, and Mr. Pierpont contributed the following ode, set to "Yankee Doodle," and couched in genuine Yankee language :

Says Jonathan, says he, "To-day.
　I will be independent,
And so my grog I'll throw away,
　And there shall be an end on 't.
Clear the house ! The 'tarnal stuff
　Sha'n't be here so handy ;
Wife has given the winds her snuff,
　So now here goes my brandy.

"And now," says Jonathan, "towards rum
  I'm desperate unforgiving ;
The tyrant never more shall come
  Into the house I live in.
Kindred spirits, too, shall in-
  To utter darkness go forth ;
Whiskey, Toddy, Julep, Gin,
  Brandy, Beer, and so forth.

"While this cold water fills my cup
  Duns dare not assail me ;
Sheriffs shall not lock me up,
  Nor my neighbor bail me.
Lawyers will I never let
  Choose me as defendant ;
Till to death I pay my debt
  I will be independent."

The Best that I Can.

"I CANNOT do much," said a little star,
  "To make the dark world bright ;
My silver beams cannot struggle far
  Through the folding gloom of night !
But I am a part of God's great plan,
And I'll cheerfully do the best that I can."

"What is the use," said a fleecy cloud,
  "Of these dewdrops that I hold ?
They will hardly bend the lily proud,
  Though caught in her cup of gold ;
Yet I am a part of God's great plan ;
My treasures I'll give as well as I can."

A child went merrily forth to play,
  But a thought, like a silver thread,
Kept winding in and out all day
  Through the happy, busy head :
"Mother said, 'Darling, do all you can,
For you are a part of God's great plan.'"

So she helped a younger child along,
  When the road was rough to the feet ;
And she sang from her heart a little song,
  A song that was passing sweet ;
And her father, a weary, toil-worn man,
Said, "I also will do the best that I can."

Drive the Nail.

DRIVE the nail aright, boys,
  Hit it on the head ;
Strike with all your might, boys,
  While the iron's red.
Lessons you're to learn, boys,
  Study with a will ;
They who reach the top, boys,
  First must climb the hill.

Standing at the foot, boys,
  Gazing at the sky,
How can you get up, boys,
  If you never try ?
Though you stumble oft, boys,
  Never be downcast ;
Try and try again, boys :
  You'll succeed at last.

Ever persevere, boys,
  Though your task is hard ;
Toil and happy cheer, boys,
  Bring their own reward.
Never give it up, boys,
  Always say you'll try ;
Joy will fill your cup, boys,
  Flowing by and by.

Recitation for the Close of a Meeting.

DEAR friends, we hope what has been said to-night
  some good will do ;
'Tis not for mere amusement our pieces we've gone
  through.
We wish to get both old and young to join the temperance cause,
To put the drinking customs down, and drunkard-
  making laws.

'Tis said that sixty thousand souls each year by drink
  are slain,
And God's Word says the drunkard's doom is ever-
  lasting pain ;
Oh ! think of this, ye moderate men who take a glass
  or two :
These poor inebriates once began with little drops, like
  you.

Oh ! think of all the drink-cursed homes—of little
  children there,
Who never sing sweet hymns of praise or breathe a
  simple prayer ;
But roam about the streets at will, ill clad, ill fed, un-
  taught,
Until, by bad companions led, to some bad end they're
  brought.

Do let us see, before we part, that we some good have
    done ;
All you who have not signed the pledge, come, sign it
    every one,
And then with all these liquors successfully you'll
    cope,
And God will smile upon our work and bless our Band
    of Hope.

_____

Good Advice from a Young Adviser.

" BE sure you are right, and then go ahead."
As soon as you're sleepy, run straight off to bed.

Before you speak crossly, or act very naughty,
Go look in the glass long enough to count forty.

Don't swear, chew, or steal, and be kind to the poor,
And wipe your feet clean when you enter the door.

_____

A Boy's Resolve.
T. R. THOMPSON.

WHAT ! drink the drunkard's drink ?
    No, sir, I will never ;
For I've signed the temperance pledge,
    And I'll keep it ever.

What ! tamper with the nation's curse,
    Barter health and reason,
Break a sacred, solemn vow ?
    That, sir, would be treason.

What ! blight my parents' hopes,
    Life's endearments sever,
Nurse a serpent in my breast ?
    No, sir, that I'll never !

What ! break the temperance pledge ?
No, not if I know it.
'Tis the safeguard of my youth ;
Firm support I owe it.

Prevention or Cure—which?

JOHN B. GOUGH.

"PREVENTION is better than cure." It is a great
work to save a drunkard. It is worth a life-effort to
lift a man from degradation. It is worth a mighty
self-sacrifice to lift a man up and enable him to stand
as *a man*, shaken free from his debasement and his
fetters. But to prevent his fall is far better.

A boy when asked, "Would you tell a lie for fifty
dollars ?" replied, "No ; because when the dollars are
gone the lie will stick." Though we may reform a
man from drunkenness, no one can ever fully recover
from the effects of years of dissipation and intemperance. You put your hand in the hand of a giant, and
he crushes it. You shriek in your agony, and by and
by, with a desperate effort, you draw forth your hand.
It is crushed, and torn, and mangled, and bleeding.
That hand may be at last healed ; but it will be a mu-
tilated hand as long as you live. And so a man may
be cured of this evil of drunkenness ; but the marks
are upon him, and will be to the day of his death.
Therefore it is a greater work to prevent than it is to
cure, and prevention is the work in which we are en-
gaged.

No one would suppose that there would be opposition to this work ; but there are some persons who
oppose everything that does not suit their own narrow
views, or that they themselves have not suggested, and
so there is opposition. The great objection seems to be

that these children are led and enticed to sign the
pledge without appealing to their understanding. Sir
Walter Scott once said : "It is all folly to talk of
writing down to the capacity of children. Give them
something to grasp after, and they will grasp that
which will astonish you." We often hear shrewd remarks from children, and we call them "haphazard,"
but they are not.

I knew two boys very well. One of them was about
ten years old. His name was Willie and the other's
was Jamie. Jamie was seated on a doorstep whittling
a stick, as Yankee boys do. The other boy, Willie,
had caught a fly, and, holding it in his fingers, he
said : "What a queer thing a fly is, isn't it ? Just
look at its legs. Look at its wings. When I blow
him he'll buzz ! An't it queer ? I wonder how God
made him." *That* has been a wonder to many. Pro-
fessor Huxley cannot answer that question. No sci-
entist can. "Jamie, how do you suppose God made a
fly ?" The little fellow, whittling away at his stick,
said : "Why, Willie, God don't make things as carpen-
ters makes things—putting on 'em together and a-fit-
ting of 'em. God says, 'Let there be flies,' and then
there is flies.'" Call that "haphazard"? No ! That
boy had heard or read the sublime passage, "God said,
Let there be light, and there was light." And thence
he reasoned out the creative power of the Almighty.

My Sentiments.

(*FOR A LITTLE BOY.*)

MRS. R. B. W. CRAFTS.

I BELIEVE in being social !
  If a brother man you meet,
Just say a kind and friendly word
  While passing up the street.

And if a stranger comes this way,
  Be sure you don't forget
To make him *feel* 'twas good for him
  That you and he had met.

Has a brother or a sister
  Fallen in the slough of sin ?
Why, lend a hand to pull them out,
  Don't push them farther in.

God has put *sunshine* in your heart ;
  Just let it shine and play
For every one, in church or street,
  Who happens in your way.

The Boys We Want.

A. SARGENT.

BOYS, we want you—OUR COUNTRY wants
  True-hearted, noble boys,
To make your world a happier place,
  To purify its joys ;
To stand among the leaders
  Of every righteous cause,
To spread o'er all the nation
  Right, just, and blessèd laws.

Boys, we want you—PATRIOTS call
  You to the conflict now ;
Beneath the yoke of fashion's power
  See millions daily bow.
There are hearts with grief o'erflowing ;
  Let us cheer them, if we can.
Come and help to burst the fetters
  Which surround your fellow-man.

Boys, we want you—TEMPERANCE wants
    Firm, consistent lives to-day ;
Victory marks her glorious progress,
    Homes are bright beneath her sway.
Shall the drunkard, lost for ever
    In despair and anguish, die ?
Let us take the pledge to save him—
    All together—you and I.

Boys, we want you—JESUS wants
    Your hearts His truth to spread ;
Follow Him in storm and sunshine,
    Ever in His footsteps tread.
There's a world of light and beauty ;
    This is not the traveller's home :
We are pressing on to Zion,
    And we want you all to come.

Boys, we want you—GLORY wants
    Every one her crown to wear ;
Each soul we've happier made on earth
    Will increase its lustre there.
Time is flying, dashing onward ;
    Soon our day's work must be done ;
And an earnest, prayerful life, boys,
    Is eternity begun.

What I Think.

I THINK that every mother's son,
    And every father's daughter,
Should drink, at least till twenty-one,
    Just nothing but cold water ;
And after that they might drink tea,
    But nothing any stronger.
If all folks would agree with me
    They'd live a great deal longer.

Dare to Stand Alone.

BE firm, be bold, be strong, be true,
  And dare to stand alone ;
Stand for the right whate'er ye do,
  Though helpers there be none.

Nay, bend not to the swelling surge
  Of popular sneer and wrong ;
'Twill bear thee on to ruin's verge
  With current wild and strong. .

Stand for the right ! Humanity
  Implores, with groans and tears,
Thine aid to break the festering links
  That bind her toiling years.

Stand for the right ! Though falsehood reign,
  And proud lips coldly sneer,
A poisoned arrow cannot wound
  A conscience pure and clear.

Stand for the right, and with clean hands
  Exalt the truth on high !
Thou'lt find warm, sympathizing hearts
  Among the passers-by—

Men who have seen, and thought, and felt,
  And yet could hardly dare
The battle's brunt, but by thy side
  Will every danger share.

Stand for the right ! proclaim it loud !
  Thou'lt find an answering tone
In honest hearts, and thou no more
  Be doomed to stand alone.

Nothing but Leaves.

"NOTHING but leaves "—the words came low,
In saddened tones so full of woe ;
My heart with anguish then was stirred,
While to my ears there came a word—
   Tobacco.

"Nothing but leaves "—yet many a slave
Has early filled the drunkard's grave,
And sadly owned the tempter's power,
And cursed the day and cursed the hour
   When first he used tobacco.

"Tobacco is a poison weed,
It was the devil who sowed the seed; "
To raise a crop of gin and rum,
Dear friends, I think, most every one
   Commences with tobacco.

"Nothing but leaves," yet something more
When once we see the dreadful power
It has upon the sons of men
Who chew and smoke, and chew again,
   The filthy weed—tobacco.

A slave to just a few poor leaves,
No matter whose dear heart it grieves—
Whoever is a slave like this
Can never find in endless bliss
   A place for his tobacco.

In heaven tobacco has no place,
On earth it is a foe to grace ;
And the devil, who sowed the seed,
Will say : " Come home, slaves of the weed,
   My harvest from tobacco."

High-Top Boots.

[We do not know the name of the writer of the first three verses of this poem, but Mr. Edward Carswell has added the fourth verse, which makes it a capital recitation for a little boy. He must have on a pair of new boots, frequently look proudly down on them, and, with his hands in his pockets, walk around as he recites. Select the smallest boy who can recite well.]

You'd better not call me Captain Boots,
   I've grown too big for that ;
It is time that I played with girls no more,
   And I think that I'll drop the cat.
Old hen, if you snap your spurs at me
You will have to stand a fight with three—
A couple of boots and a man, do you see ?
   Ho ! pretty good boots ! Ho ! high-top boots,
   Ho ! gentleman's boots for me.

Stand out of the way, I'm going to walk ;
   I'll tread on somebody soon.
Oh ! how they do squeak. Yes, how they talk !
   I think it is good as a tune.
They tie themselves without any strings,
They match like a pair of angel's wings.
New leather ! I hope you smell the things.
   Ho ! pretty good boots ! Ho ! high-top boots,
   Ho ! gentleman's boots for me.

I wish it was Sunday to go to church,
   I wish it was Monday to play,
I wish it was Tuesday to ride my horse—
   I wish it was every day.
I will wear them to bed, for Uncle Jim
Might fill them with water up to the brim,
As once I filled his boots for him.
   Ho ! pretty good boots ! Ho ! high-top boots,
   Ho ! gentleman's boots for me.

They're temperance boots, for I wore them first
    To the Band of Hope last night,
And they squeaked so loud that the chairman said
    That he thought they must be *tight;*
But they're *temperance* boots, and would just as
    soon
Think of walking straight up to the moon
As of walking into a drink-saloon.
    Ho ! pretty good boots ! Ho ! high-top boots,
    Ho ! *teetotal* boots for me.

A Little Talk on a Big Subject.

I AM a little fellow, but I am going to talk about a big subject. 'Tis not too big for such as we are, either. Some men laugh about little boys and girls forming cold-water armies. "What good can *you* do ?" Let me tell you. You have heard of a little mouse that a lion helped out of a little trouble, and laughed at him because he said something about returning the favor. Well, the great lion was caught in a hunter's net, and he roared and growled and bit ; this was all he could do. By and by the little mouse came along and gnawed off, one by one, the cords of the great net, and let the lion go. That is what we mean to do. We may be very little mice, but we mean to gnaw off every cord of the great net that has bound down our country for so many years. The net is intemperance, and our cold-water pledge can cut off all the deceiving threads that work so pleasingly, as wine, beer, and cider, as well as the stouter cords, rum, gin, and brandy. Now, don't you think we can do something ? We know we can. Intemperance sha'n't catch *us*, at any rate.

The Independent Man.

MRS. M. A. KIDDER.

I STAND before you, one and all,
To sound aloud the temperance call,
And picture out, sirs, if I can,
The real independent man—
    The independent man !

He neither smokes, nor drinks, nor chews ;
The glass he firmly can refuse ;
He lives not under terror's ban ;
He is an independent man—
    An independent man !

By living right he garners health,
He makes good friends and garners wealth.
The charms of nature he can scan
With joy, this independent man—
    This independent man !

He counts his home a place of rest ;
His wife and children wear the best ;
No drunken temper mars the plan
Of this our independent man—
    Our independent man !

The tempter finds him all prepared ;
His good right arm is ever bared.
To victory he leads the van,
This very independent man—
    This independent man !

He who resolved with all his soul
To dash to earth the " flowing bowl "
Has been, e'er since the world began,
The REAL independent man—
    The independent man !

My First Speech.

You'd scarce expect one of my age
To plead for temperance on the stage ;
And should I chance to fall below
Portraying all the drunkard's woe,
Don't view me with a critic's eye,
Nor pass my simple story by.

Large streams from little fountains flow ;
Great sots from moderate drinkers grow ;
And though I now am small and young,
No *rum* shall ever *touch my tongue!*

Now, where's the town, go far or near,
That sells the rum that we do here ?
Or where's the boy but three feet high
That hates the traffic worse than I ?

The Drink for You.

GEORGE W. BUNGAY.

Each flower holds a dainty cup
    To catch the rain and dew ;
Each bonny gem upon its stem
    Lets the light in and through ;
The drink of flowers, distilled in showers,
    Is just the drink for you.

The nightingale that cheers the vale
    From crystal streamlets flew
On vibrant wings, and when it sings
    Its notes are clear and true ;
The song-birds' drink should be, I think,
    The drink for birds like you.

The stars so bright that gem the night,
  Shining like diamonds through,
Are sleepless eyes, in sheltering skies,
  Glancing from curtains blue ;
They fling their beams upon the streams
  That flow with drink for you.

When Hagar prayed for rain and shade,
  A fountain rose in view,
For unseen hands had scooped the sands
  And brought the waters through ;
She wept and smiled, and gave her child
  The drink that's good for you.

Water alone, where the sun shone
  From burning skies of blue,
He drank with joy. What of the boy ?
  "A mighty man he grew."
"Better than gold is water cold "
  For boys and girls like you.

What a Little Child Can Do.

I'M a very little maid ;
  Hardly can I talk, 'tis true ;
Yet mamma I'd love to aid—
  This a little child can do !

I can go on busy feet
  Errands for her, all day through;
Work for her, I feel, is sweet—
  This a little child can do !

I can hold the great long skein
  When 'tis tangled and askew,
Never wanting to complain—
  This a little child can do !

I can talk to wicked boys,
  Tell them what is good and true,
Make them love the Sunday-school—
  This a little child can do !

Tracts on temperance I can give
  To erring men who drink and chew ;
Point out a better way to live—
  This a little child can do !

Faith, Hope, Charity.

(FOR A SMALL BOY OR GIRL.)

I HAVE a few remarks to make,
  And, that I may not waste your time,
I guess the shortest way I'll take
  And give my speech in rhyme.

I am not old enough to teach,
  But, if I live, may some time be,
And so a sermon I will preach
  On Faith, Hope, Charity.

There's Faith and Hope—I'll say to you
  I cannot, somehow, make these rhyme,
And so I guess I'll leave these two
  Until another time.

But love you must, because you can,
  And have a little bit for me ;
Let love abound—love God, love man
  And our Society.

Have faith, have hope, have charity,
  Love everybody every day,
And be as good as you can be,
  And—*that is all I have to say.*

An Address of a Young Volunteer.

FRIENDS AND FELLOW-WORKERS : I appear before you, not as a veteran, not as one who has stood in the deadly breach, but as a young soldier, devoted to a glorious cause, and determined to conquer or die on the field of battle.

Friends, let us plant ourselves on the high and holy principles of total abstinence. Let us be sure that our feet are firmly fixed, for the day is at hand which will try our patriotism and our courage. The field is opening wider and wider before us, and every day is adding to our numbers. Our minds as well as our bodies are enlarging. What we do not understand to-day we may understand to-morrow. The weapons which we cannot carry to-day we may carry next year. While our fathers and mothers are going down into the vale of years, we are toiling up its summit. Every day brings with it a more extensive prospect and a stronger eye to encompass it. Then are we not called upon to give our whole hearts to the work ? Have we not seen the drunkard go down to the grave, there to lie by the side of his wife whom his cruelty had sent there broken-hearted before him ? And does not their blood cry to us from the ground ? As we walk among the tombs does not the voice come up from many a drunkard's grave, " Go on, ye youthful heroes ! Ye cannot enlist too early in the cause of temperance. King Alcohol has planted his victims thickly around us. It is yours to wrest the weapons from his hand. Go on to victory ! "

Friends and fellow-soldiers, let us not hear that voice in vain. Hark ! there comes another. The graves of the drunkard's children, by the cold neglect or the murderous hand of those who should have protected them, bid us all " Go on ! go on ! " As for

me I answer : "I will go on ! 'Come life, come
death, my voice is still for war.'"

Water for Me.

(From *Good Times*.)

Single Voice—

    WHAT say the joyous birds
      Warbling in glee ?
    Hark to their cheerful words :
    "Water for me !"

School—Water, pure water, fresh, sparkling, and
      gushing !
Boys—   Water for me !
Girls—   Water for me !

Single Voice—

    What says the tiny flower,
      Silvered with dew,
    Unfolding every hour
    Beauties to view ?

School—Water, pure water, fresh, sparkling, and
      gushing !
Boys—   Water for me !
Girls—   Water for me !

Single Voice —

    What cries the waving grain
      Up to the sky ?
    "Give us the blessed rain
      Soon, or we die !"

School—Water, pure water, fresh, sparkling, and
      gushing !
Boys—   Water for me !
Girls—   Water for me !

Single Voice—
>   What say the girls and boys,
>   Ruddy and fair ?
>   " Give us pure, healthy joys,
>   Found only there."

School—Water, pure water, fresh, sparkling, and
     gushing !
Boys—   Water for me !
Girls—   Water for me !

Making Believe.

ELLA WHEELER.

I THINK it's true of every boy,
  Or almost every one,
To want to be a soldier
  And carry round a gun.
They like to play at fighting
  And " make believe " a war,
But I think there are some boys who know
  Just what they're fighting for.

I fight for right and principle,
  Sobriety and truth ;
My enemies are all strong drinks,
  The licensed foes of youth.
But sometimes, just for rare good fun,
  To make it lively work,
I imagine I'm a Russian
  And that cider is a *Turk.*

Again I am a border-man,
  Just ready for the strife,
And cider is an Indian,
  Who means to take my life.

You ought to see me skirmish then,
    You ought to hear me shout ;
Where'er the red foe lurks I mean
    To wholly put him out.

Ah ! boys, we need to be alive
    And ready for the work ;
For, worse than any Indian,
    More cruel than a Turk,
Our cider foe is gaining ground,
    The subtle, crafty thief !
And we must leave no stone unturned
    To bring the wretch to grief.

A Short Sermon.

MRS. M. B. C. SLADE.

I'M going to preach a sermon, and this is my text :
  "THE LORD LOVETH A CHEERFUL GIVER."

                Now, what shall I say next ?
Don't you want the Lord to love you ?   All of you who
    say *yes*
May raise the right hand.   *It is every one,* I guess.
Now we shall give you a chance in a little while to
    show
If you want the Lord to love you.   (Take the boxes,
    boys, and go.)
Be a *giver ;* give us money for the temperance cause
    to-night.
He loveth a *cheerful giver ;* give, and you'll be all
    right ;
But you must not look sober, nor selfish, nor unwill-
    ing ;
You may give just what you please, a penny or a
    shilling,

But if you want the Lord to love you, as in my text,
    you see
You must *look* and *be* as cheerful as ever you can be.
Now keep that smiling face while you find and give
    your penny—
Borrow some of your neighbor, if you forgot to bring
    any.
It is bad to find no money in your pocket or your purse,
But to *have* and not be willing to give, that is ten times
    worse !
Don't anybody look solemn, or sober, or selfish, or
    vexed ;
"The Lord loveth a *cheerful* giver "—*that* is my text.

Our Promise.

WE girls and boys
    Do not think
It wise, to taste
    The drunkard's drink.

We therefore promise
    To abstain,
And firm to temperance
    Will remain.

This pledge I take,
    And hope that I
Shall sober live
    And sober die.

The Cup-Bearer.

THE little cup-bearer entered the room
    After the banquet was done ;
His eyes were like the skies of May,
    All bright with a cloudless sun,

His hair a soft and wavy brown,
His forehead white and high,
And his gentle voice and courteous mien
Were a joy to every eye.

The little cup-bearer in his hand
Carried a silver horn,
Wherein there flashed a rare old wine
With a tint like the purple morn.
Kneeling beside his master's feet—
The feet of the noble king—
He raised the goblet : "Drink, my liege,
The offering that I bring !"

"Now, nay !" the good king, smiling, said.
"But first—a faithful sign
That thou bringest me no poison draught—
Taste thou, my page, of the wine !"
Then sweet but gravely spoke the lad :
"My dearest master, *no !*
Though at thy lightest wish my feet
Shall gladly come and go."

"Rise up, my little cup-bearer !"
The king astonished cried.
"Rise up and tell me straightway why
Is my request denied ?"
The young page rose up slowly,
With sudden paling cheek,
While all the lords and ladies
Waited to hear him speak.

"My father sat in princely halls,
And tasted wine with you :
He died a wretched drunkard, sire !"
(The brave voice tearful grew.)

"I vowed to my dear mother,
  Beside his dying-bed,
That for her sake I would not taste
  The tempting poison red !"

"Away with this young upstart !"
  The lords impatient cry ;
But, spilling slow the purple wine,
  The good king made reply :
"Thou shalt be my little cup-bearer,
  And honored well," he said ;
"But see thou bring no wine to me,
  But water pure instead !"

Tobacco.

(*A SPEECH FOR A BOY.*)

GEORGE W. BUNGAY.

I GO against tobacco because it goes against me. I
eschew it ; I will not chew it. I will tell you why.
1st. I do not like the taste of it. It tastes worse than
the bitterest medicine ever put to my lips. It is such
sickening stuff! 2d. I don't like the looks of it. In
the words of another, When I see the tobacco, I pity
the mouth that chews it ; and when I see the mouth
that chews it, I pity the tobacco. It has not a taking
color. It is of a dirty dirt color. 3d. I don't like the
effects of its use. It makes the teeth yellow and brown
when they should be white ; it makes the breath sour
and offensive when it should be sweet ; it injures the
voice, so that those who chew cannot sing and speak
to advantage. The voice breaks, and the chorister
croaks like a raven when he should sing like a bobo-
link ; the orator merely barks, and a tobacco bark is
very disagreeable. 4th. The habit of chewing is a

filthy habit. Look at the carpets, the stairways, the sitting-rooms where the chewers gather together and roll the quid like a sweet morsel under their tongue. Every one that chews ought to wear a hat shaped like a spittoon, and use it as such wherever he goes ; indeed, he ought to wear it when he sleeps; such a night-cap might save the pillow-case from stains. 5th. I fear tobacco creates an appetite for liquor. It lights a fire in the throat which water may not put out.

The House full of Wine.

BY JOHNSON BARKER.

A GAY little fly on a bright summer's morn
    Went buzzing about 'mid the clover and corn,
Till, buzzed out of breath, he sat down on a flower,
    And thought he would just take a nap for an hour.
A spider who built up a dwelling close by,
    Just wanting a morsel to make up a pie,
Looking out of his window, delightedly sees
    This fat little fly coolly taking his ease.
So he let himself down with his pulley and thread
    Till he came to a leaf that was over his head,
And, speaking as kindly as ever he could,
    Began to persuade him he'd come for his good.

" My dear little fly," said the spider above,
    " I've a house full of wine and a heart full of love;
You're welcome to both, and I've just come to say
    How glad I shall be of a visit to-day.
I fear you'll take cold from the damp of this flower;
    There's room in my house, and I dine in an hour.
Take hold of my arm, you have nothing to fear;
    I'll give you the best, both of welcome and cheer."

So the poor little fly, with a nod of his head,
  Bowed, smiled, and consented to do as he said;
And smacking his lips at the thought of the wine,
  Went up with the spider to rest and to dine.

Up a street and an alley of lilies and grass;
  Bees, butterflies, crickets start up as they pass,
And a small lady-bird ran to hide in a rose,
  For fear the great spider should tread on her toes.
To his mansion he came; it was knitted with thread,
  And built upon briers, with leaves overhead.
Without ringing the bell or tapping the door
  They enter at once on the back parlor floor;
And the fly, seizing hold of a king-cup of wine,
  When he'd swallowed it down, really thought it
    so fine
That a blue bottle full by his side on the floor
  He drained at a breath, and then asked for some
    more.

He drank the drink till he suddenly found
  That spider and king-cups were all turning round,
And, alarmed, he'd at once have been off like a shot,
  But he found that his feet were enchained to the
    spot.
"O good Mr. Spider! unfasten my feet,"
  Said the fly, "for I've a lady to meet;
Oh! don't look so fierce—I'm dizzy and queer.
  Pray, pray let me go! I've been long enough
    here."
'Twas all of no use, for the poor little fly
  Was killed by the spider to make up his pie—
A bee who was passing at twelve heard his groans,
  And a cricket at night saw the ants at his bones.

There are men, like the spider, who " make up their
pies "
By luring their fellows and blinding their eyes ;
They tempt them with drink till they've come to dis-
grace,
And fasten their feet, like the fly's, to the place.
They build up their webs, both in country and town,
To catch high and low, from the lord to the clown;
There are inns for the rich, and shops for the poor,
Full of wine, gin, and rum, to attract and allure.
They'll perhaps talk to you of " their house full of
wine,"
And tempt you with that to come in and dine;
But *beware!* and take care by the fate of the fly,
For be sure they but want you to "make up their
pie."

Something to Hate.

I LOVE the luscious grapes that cling
In clusters on the vine—
Bright groups of *neckless bottles* filled
With nature's harmless wine.
But when, despoiled of all their charms,
They fall to low estate,
Their sweetness into poison turned,
I've something then to hate !

I love the apples, blushing 'neath
The sun's too ardent rays ;
They bring me pleasant memories of
Dear childhood's happy days.
But when, by "Folly's" hand transformed,
They lure and fascinate,
Their harmlessness and beauty gone,
I've something then to hate !

I love the graceful barley, which,
  Disguised in beard of gold,
Goes flirting with the zephyrs like
  A cavalier of old ;
But when the cruel hand of art
  Doth such a change create
That wholesome food's to poison turned,
  I've something then to hate.

What I Like.

ELLA WHEELER.

If there's anything I hate to see,
It's a little boy, like you or me,
His hat tipped over upon one side,
Swelling along with a strut and a stride ;

Puffing away at an old cigar,
Or a nasty pipe that's worse by far,
His cheek puffed out with a filthy cud,
Poisoning all his pure young blood ;

Talking slang in a swaggering way,
Or swearing when he has much to say,
And striving, in every way he can,
To make folks think he's a grown-up man.

But I'll tell you what I like to see,
And what I strive myself to be :
A merry, cheerful, boyish boy,
Brimming over with fun and joy ;

Who knows and is glad that he is young,
Who lets no oaths pollute his tongue,
Who don't use tobacco in any way,
Who tries to learn something new each day ;

Who expects in time to walk with men,
But is willing to be a boy till then ;
And a boy who rejoices in his youth,
Who hates low things and loves the truth.

Yes ! that is the boy I like to see,
And that is what I will strive to be;
And I think it safer and better far
Than swearing and smoking an old cigar.

The Reason Why.

(FOR WASHINGTON'S BIRTHDAY.)

A BOSTON master said one day,
"Boys, tell me, if you can, I pray,
Why Washington's birthday should shine
In to-day's history more than mine ?"

At once such stillness in the hall
You might have heard a feather fall ;
Exclaims a boy not three feet high,
" Because *he* never told a lie!"

Only One.

ONLY one ! That is the reason
  You should strive to do your best.
Never mind your neighbor's duties;
  Do your own and leave the rest.

You are only one ; then ever,
  Ever till your life is done,
Bravely, earnestly, and kindly
  Try to do the work of one.

Though your story be not written
Brightly on the scroll of fame ;
Though unknown your place of resting,
And forgotten e'en your name,

Yet the world will still be better
For the life-task you have done,
If with true and earnest spirit
You will do the work of one.

Our Model Man.

JULIA COLMAN.

WOULD you like to know what kind of a man we are
going to take for our model ? It is not the reformed
man, though we are glad he reformed. We wish all
the drinking men would reform. But we don't mean
to be reformed men when we grow up, because, you see,
we do not mean to drink. The man that we propose to
copy after is the man that never drank a single glass
of intoxicating liquors in all his life. Do you know
any such man ? I think may be you might find one
or two right around here. Any way, I am sure it can
be done. The Bible tells us about one man that did it,
and that was Samuel. And there is another man that
has done it. He lives in the northern part of the State
of New York. He is one hundred and two years old.
I don't know as I shall live to be so old as that, but I
am sure I should live longer without drink than I
should with it. Any way, while I do live I should
like to glory in the fact that I never drank intoxicating liquors. Boys, how many of you will strike hands
with me on that, and take for your model the man
that never drank ?

Caw! Caw! Caw!

EDWARD CARSWELL.

The effect is very comical if the "caws" are well mimicked.

CAW ! caw ! caw !
I am a poor old crow !
And I just want to know
　Why you treat us with cruelty and scorn ?
　Caw ! caw ! caw !   .
Why you shoot us with a gun,
And seem to think it fun,
　If we just take a grain or two of corn ?

Caw ! caw ! caw !
Yet you'll make it into drink,
Which does more harm, I think,
　Than all the crows that ever flew in air;
　Caw ! caw ! caw !
For *it* blights where'er it flows,
Killing men instead of crows.
　Then why not *eat*, and let *us* have a share ?
　Caw ! caw ! caw !

Beware of " Crooked Whiskey."

MRS. M. A. KIDDER.

OF all the crooked things in life
To breed distemper, care, and strife,
　The crookedest is whiskey.
For those who drink it day by day
There is no "straight and narrow way ";
By devious winding paths they stray.
　Beware of crooked whiskey !

A man may be as upright, sir,
As yonder poplar, ash, or fir ;
    But let him take to whiskey,
And you will see, my watchful friend,
His blood will turn, his back will bend,
And "crooked " fancies prove his end—
    And all by drinking whiskey.

The drunkard's wife and children know
Such crooked facts in homes of woe ;
    They hate the name of whiskey.
In crooked paths their shoeless feet
Go wearily from street to street,
And scanty is the bread they eat,
    And all by crooked whiskey.

        Beware, beware, my friends, beware !
        Don't do a thing so risky
        As breeding strife and shortening life
        By drinking crooked whiskey.

Who Killed Tom Roper?

MRS. C. H. OBEAR.

WHO killed Tom Roper ?
Not I, said New Cider ;
I couldn't kill a spider—
    I didn't kill Tom Roper.

Not I, said Strong Ale ;
I make men tough and hale—
    I didn't kill Tom Roper.

Not I, said Lager-Beer ;
I don't intoxicate. D'ye hear ?   [Cross.]
    I didn't kill Tom Roper.

Not I, said Bourbon Whiskey ;
I make sick folks spry and frisky ;
The doctors say so—don't they know
What quickens blood that runs so slow ?
   I didn't kill Tom Roper.

Not I, said sparkling old Champagne :
No poor man e'er by me was slain ;
I cheer the rich in lordly halls,
And scorn the place where the drunkard
   falls—
   I didn't kill Tom Roper.

Not we, said various other wines.
What ! juice of grapes, product of vines,
Kill a man ! The Bible tells
That wine all other drinks excels—
   We didn't kill Tom Roper.

Not I, said Holland Gin ;
To charge such a crime to me is sin—
   I didn't kill Tom Roper.

Not I, spoke up the Brandy strong ;
He grew too poor to buy me long—
   I didn't kill Tom Roper.

Not I, said Medford Rum ;   ·
He was almost gone before I come—
   I didn't kill Tom Roper.

Ha ! ha ! laughed old Prince Alcohol :
Each struck the blow that made him fall ;
And all that helped to make him toper
My agents were to kill Tom Roper.

THE

JUVENILE TEMPERANCE RECITER:

A COLLECTION

OF

RECITATIONS AND DECLAMATIONS,

IN PROSE AND VERSE,

FOR USE IN

BANDS OF HOPE, JUVENILE TEMPLES, TEMPERANCE
SCHOOLS, SUNDAY-SCHOOLS, AND ALL
JUVENILE ORGANIZATIONS.

NEW YORK:
The National Temperance Society and Publication House,
58 READE STREET.

—

1880.

New Temperance Dialogues.

THE NATIONAL TEMPERANCE SOCIETY has just published three new dialogues, written by H. Elliott McBride:

1. **A Boy's Rehearsal,** for eight boys, in which each one rehearses his speech selected for a public meeting. This is one of the best temperance dialogues for boys ever published. 18mo, 20 pages, **10 cents;** single copies, per dozen **$1.00**
2. **A Talk on Temperance,** for two boys, an earnest effort for recruits for a public meeting. 18mo, 7 pages, **6 cents** single copies; per dozen .... **.60**
3. **A Bitter Dose,** two characters, man and wife. The drunkard cured by a "bitter dose." 18mo, 14 pages, **10 cents** single copies; per dozen. **1.00**

The following has also Recently been Published.

4. **Trial of John Barleycorn,** by a Jury of twelve men, with Attorney-General, Counsel, Sheriffs. and fifteen Witnesses, **10 cents** each; per dozen... **1.00**

The following are Excellent Dialogues previously published.

Marry No Man if He Drinks. 10 cents ....Per dozen		1.00
Which will You Choose ? By Miss M. D. Chellis. 15 cents.	"	1.50
Wine as a Medicine. 10 cents	"	1.00
The Stumbling Block. 10 cents......................	"	1.00
Shall I Marry a Moderate Drinker ? 10 cents........	"	1.00
Trial and Condemnation of Judas Woemaker. 15 cents	"	1.50
The First Glass; or. The Power of Woman's Influence, and ⟩	"	
The Young Teetotaler; or, Saved at Last. 15 cents for both. ⟨	"	1.50
Reclaimed; or, The Danger of Moderate Drinking. 10 cents.	"	1.00
The Alcohol Fiend. 5 cents......................	"	.60

CONCERT EXERCISES.

The Two Ways. By George Thayer. 5 cents each ....Per dozen		.60
The Cup of Death. By Rev. W. F. Crafts. 5 cents each..	"	.60
The Two Wines. By T. R. Thompson. 5 cents each.....	"	.60
The Alcohol Fiend. By Rev. W. F. Crafts. 5 cents each.	"	.60
Temperance Exercise. By Edward Clark. 18mo......	"	.60
Scripture Testimony. By T. R. Thompson. 5 cts. each..	"	.60
Beware of Strong Drink. By Mrs. E. H. Thompson. 5 cts. each............................	"	.60
The Contrast. By T. R. Thompson. 3 cents each......	"	.36
The Fruits Thereof. By T. R. Thompson. 5 cents each.	"	.60
Scripture Characters. By T. R. Thompson. 5 cents each.	"	.60

AMONG THE CHILDREN.

The Catechism on Alcohol. By Miss Julia Colman. 36 pages....................................	"	.60
Band of Hope Manual. 36 pages	"	.60
Chromo Pledge Card. Containing either the single or triple pledge.......................per hundred		2.00
Pocket Pledge-Book. With space for 80 names.		.10
The Temperance Speaker. By J. N. Stearns. 288 pages.........		.75
The National Temperance Orator. By Miss L. Penney. 12mo, 288 pages........................		1.00
Ripples of Song. 64 pages. Single copies, 15 cents .. per hundred		12.00

A new collection of Temperance Hymns and Songs. designed for children and youth in Sabbath-schools, Bands of Hope, Juvenile Templars, Cadets of Temperance, etc.

Readings and Recitations, Nos. 1 and 2. 96 pages. By Miss L. Penney. Each.. **.25**

Address **J. N. STEARNS, Publishing Agent,**
58 Reade Street, New York.

FOR SUNDAY-SCHOOL LIBRARIES.

THE NATIONAL TEMPERANCE SOCIETY AND PUBLICATION HOUSE have published ninety-eight books specially adapted to Sunday-school Libraries, which have been carefully examined and approved by a Publication Committee of twelve representing the various religious denominations, and they have been highly recommended by numerous ecclesiastical bodies and temperance organizations all over the land. They should be in every Sunday-school library. The following is the list, any of which can be ordered through any bookseller, or direct from the rooms of the Society, 58 Reade Street, New York:

At Lion's Mouth	$1 25	Jug-or-Not	$1 25
Adopted	60	Little Girl in Black	90
Andrew Douglas	75	Life Cruise of Captain Bess Adams,	
Aunt Dinah's Pledge	1 25	The	1 50
Alice Grant	1 25	McAllisters, The	50
All for Money	1 25	Mill and the Tavern, The	1 25
Brewery at Taylorville, The	1 50	Model Landlord, The	60
Barford Mills	1 00	More Excellent Way, A	1 00
Best Fellow in the World, The	1 25	Mr. Mackenzie's Answer	1 25
Broken Rock, The	50	National Temperance Orator, The,	1 00
Brook, and the Tide Turning, The,	1 00	Nettie Loring	1 25
Brewer's Fortune, The	1 50	No Danger	1 25
Caught and Fettered	1 00	Norman Brill's Life Work	1 00
Circled by Fire	40	Nothing to Drink	1 50
Come Home, Mother	50	Old Times	1 25
Coals of Fire	1 00	On London Bridge	40
Curse and the Cure, The	40	Our Coffee-Room	1 00
Curse of Mill Valley, The	1 25	Old Brown Pitcher, The	1005
Drinking-Fountain Stories, The	1 00	Out of the Fire	1 25
Dumb Traitor, The	1 25	Our Parish	75
Emerald Spray, The	40	Packington Parish, and the Diver's	
Eva's Engagement Ring	90	Daughter	1 25
Echo Bank	85	Paul Brewster and Son	1 00
Esther Maxwell's Mistake	1 00	Philip Eckert's Struggles and Tri-	
Fanny Percy's Knight Errant	1 00	umphs	60
Fatal Dower, The	60	Piece of Silver, A	50
Firebrands	1 25	Pitcher of Cool Water, The	50
Fire Fighters, The	1 25	Pledge and the Cross, The	1 00
Fred's Hard Fight	1 25	Queer Home in Rugby Court, The,	1 50
Frank Spencer's Rule of Life	50	Rachel Noble's Experience	90
Frank Oldfield ; or, Lost and		Red Bridge, The	90
Found	1 50	Rev. Dr. Willoughby and his Wine,	1 50
From Father to Son	1 25	Ripley Parsonage	1 25
Gertie's Sacrifice ; or, Glimpses at		Rosa Leighton; or, In His Strength,	90
Two Lives	50	Roy's Search ; or, Lost in the Cars,	1 25
Glass Cable, The	1 25	Saved	1 25
Harry the Prodigal	1 25	Silver Castle	1 25
Hard Master, The	85	Seymours, The	1 00
Harker Family, The	1 25	Strange Sea Story, A	1 50
His Honor the Mayor	1 25	Temperance Doctor, The	1 25
History of a Threepenny Bit	75	Temperance Speaker, The	75
History of Two Lives, The	50	Temperance Anecdotes	1 00
Hopedale Tavern, and What it		Time Will Tell	1 00
Wrought	1 00	Tim's Troubles	1 50
Hole in the Bag, and other Stories,		Tom Blinn's Temperance Society,	
The	1 00	and Other Stories	1 25
How Could he Escape?	1 25	Ten Cents	1 25
Humpy Dumpy	1 25	Vow at the Bars	40
Image Unveiled, The	1 00	Wealth and Wine	1 25
Jewelled Serpent, The	1 00	White Rose, The	1 25
John Bentley's Mistake	50	Wife's Engagement Ring, The	1 25
Job Tufton's Rest	1 25	Work and Reward	50
Joe's Partner	50	Zoa Rodman	1 00

Any of the above will be sent by mail, post-paid, *on receipt of price.*

J. N. STEARNS, Publishing Agent, 58 Reade St., N. Y.